FIND THE ANIMAL

GOD MADE SOMETHING STRONG

This parrot knows what animal we're looking for. Can you find this parrot in the book?

PENNY REEVE
ILLUSTRATED BY ROGER DE KLERK
CF4•K

Let's go on an adventure, what will we find? It is something that God has made. It is something strong!

Can you find the lion?

Who is the King of Glory? The Lord strong and mighty. Psalm 24:8

Where is the green snake?

What is this? It's a foot. What is it hiding behind? God gave this animal big strong feet.

Can you find a yellow flower?

The joy of the Lord is your strength.
Nehemiah 8:10

Who has a yellow T-Shirt?

What could this be? It's an ear. How many ears can you see? God made these strong ears. These ears flap all day in order to keep cool.

Can you find the leopard?

I have heard that you O God are strong, and ... loving.
Psalm 62:11-12

Where are the green palm trees?

What about this? It's a nose. What is it doing? This nose is strong for lifting. It's also made for drinking through! God made this nose very long.

Can you find the giraffe?

Their Redeemer is strong. The Lord Almighty is his name.
Jeremiah 50:34

Who has a purple teddy-bear?

What is that? It's a tail. How many tails can you see? God gave this big, strong animal a tiny, little tail.

Can you find the parrot?

The Lord is my strength and my song. He has become my salvation.
Exodus 15:2

Who has a purple bag?

What is that? It's a tusk. What colour is it? God gave this animal strong and powerful tusks for moving earth and trees and other things.

Can you find the monkey?

I love you, O Lord, my strength. Psalm 18:1

Where is the blue striped snake?

What have we found? It is an elephant. Who made it? Our great God! An elephant is strong but God is stronger. He is so strong that nothing can separate us from his love.

Can you find the zebra?

Nothing can separate us from the love of God in Christ Jesus. Romans 8:39

Where is the grey hippo?

Thank you Jesus for being so strong!
Thank you for saving me and for loving me.

Jesus said, 'Love each other as I have loved you.'
John 15:1